For Jason, my forever friend
~ CF

For Ruth, Johnny and Anna, with all my love
~ BC

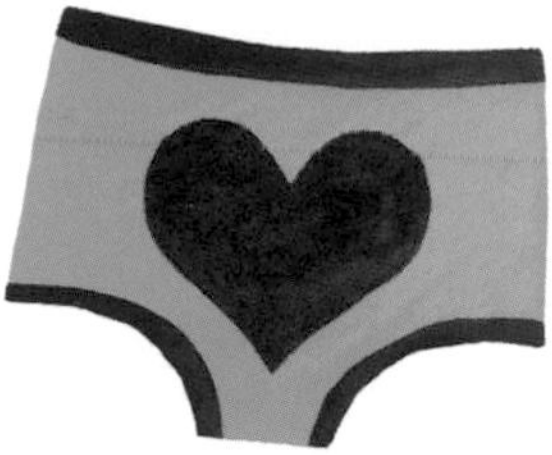

SIMON & SCHUSTER

First published in Great Britain in 2007 by Simon & Schuster UK Ltd
1st Floor, 222 Gray's Inn Road, London WC1X 8HB
A CBS COMPANY

This edition published 2017

A CIP catalogue record for this book is available from the British Library upon request

ISBN: 978-1-4711-6333-3

Printed in China

1 3 5 7 9 10 8 6 4 2

Aliens Love Underpants

Claire Freedman & Ben Cort

SIMON & SCHUSTER
London New York Sydney Toronto New Delhi

Aliens love underpants,
of every shape and size.

But there are no underpants in space,
so here's a big surprise . . .

When aliens fly down to Earth,
they don't come to meet YOU . . .

They simply want your underpants.
I'll bet you never knew!

Their spaceship's radar bleeps and blinks
the moment that it sees

a washing line of underpants,
all flapping in the breeze.

They land in your back garden,
though they haven't been invited.

'Oooooh, underpants!' they chant,
and dance around, delighted.

They like them red, they like them green,
or orange like satsumas.

But best of all they love the sight
of Granny's spotted bloomers!

Mum's pink frilly knickers
are a perfect place to hide.

And Grandpa's woolly long-johns
make a super-whizzy slide.

In daring competitions
held up by just one peg,

they count how many aliens
can squeeze inside each leg.

They wear pants on their feet and heads and other silly places.

They fly pants from their spaceships
and hold Upside-Down-Pant races!

As they go zinging through the air, it really is pants-tastic.
What fun the aliens can have, with pingy pants elastic!

It's not your neighbour's naughty dog,
or next-door's funny game.

When underpants go missing,
the ALIENS are to blame!

But quick! Mum's coming out to fetch the washing in at last.

Wheee! Off the aliens all zoom!
They're used to leaving fast . . .

So when you put your pants on,
freshly washed and nice and clean,

just check in case an alien
still lurks inside, unseen!

Ready for more alien adventures?
Check out the next pants-tastic tale . . .

. . . plus the whole Underpants series!